T0198754

Princess Leah Tutu

by

L. Simmons Lee

To order additional copies of this book, contact:
Xlibris
844-714-8691
www.Xlibris.com
Orders@Xlibris.com

ISBN: Softcover   978-1-6641-5632-6
         EBook   978-1-6641-5631-9

Print information available on the last page

Rev. date: 02/04/2021

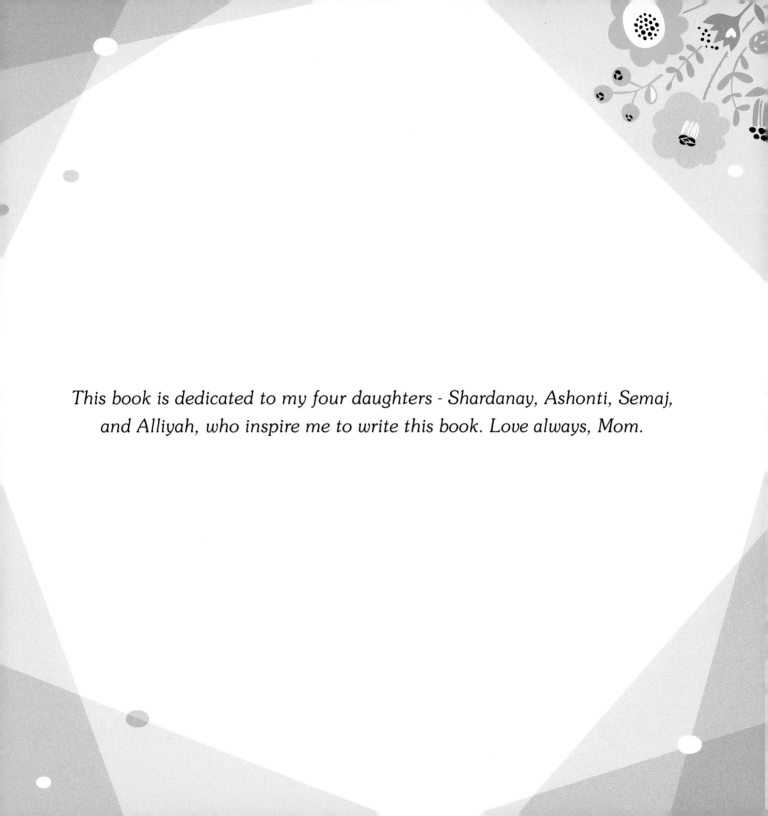

This book is dedicated to my four daughters - Shardanay, Ashonti, Semaj, and Alliyah, who inspire me to write this book. Love always, Mom.

*O*nce upon a time there was a princess named Leah. She loved unicorns and tutu's. One day a purple troll took all of Princess Leah tutu's. Princess was very sad crying in the forest.

Crunch yum crunch, what was that said

the princess is someone here? It is I Freddy the frog, are you crying? Yes,

someone took all of my beautiful tutu's. Without them I'm afraid I'll just

be plain ole Princess Leah. Stop your crying, we will find your tutu's or

my name isn't Freddy the finder that's what my name is by the way. If you

find my tutu's Freddy the finder, I will see that you are knighted by the

King. Knighted shouted Freddy no thanks I just want to help a pretty Princess

In need, that's thanks enough.

Now let's start at the beginning. Well said the

Princess, I woke up this morning to an awful smell and opened my eyes and I

thought I saw a purple hat in the shadows. A purple hat you say hmmm, sounds

familiar. Whatever do you mean said Princess Leah tutu. It started several weeks

ago that lots of thing kept on disappearing.

I remember as if it was yesterday.

The shoe maker started losing some shoes. Buckley the bread maker lost some

Bread from his window. Lacey the dressmaker stockings and ribbon's all

disappeared.

They all said the same thing that you said, a purple hat and an awful smell.

Mr. Buckley's bread

OPEN

Lacey's Boutique

SHOE
SHOP

I wonder could this be the same troll Louie the looter. Louie the looter said Princess Tutu. Yes, said Freddy. Louie has the stickiest hands alive. Let's set a trap said Freddy. How do we set a trap said the princess? We are going to make the prettiest tutu ever and put on display in your window for all to see. Yes, that sounds good and we will wait and see if Louie take the bait. Oh he Will and when we catch him we will make return all of the things that he took from others. Now you are thinking Princess, let's get started on that beautiful and outstanding tutu. Freddy we have to use our heads because Louie stole just about everything and I'm afraid I don't have much to spare. Fear not my dear let's go back to the castle and see what we can come up with now off we go princess.

Freddy and princess Leah Tutu went back to the castle

to see what they can use to make this grand tutu. I have nothing but these old

dresses and stockings.

That's good look for more princess look for much more.

Let's make it sparkle, I need jewels princess shinny bobbles ok said princess.

I need thread and a needle and come princess here we go. With the old dresses laces and jewels they came up with the most gorgeous tutu of all times. It was a site for sore eyes, wow! Freddy this great better than the tutu's that were taking from me. I love it, together we did a great job. Yes, princess we did it now let go set this trap. So they set the tutu in the window for all to see.

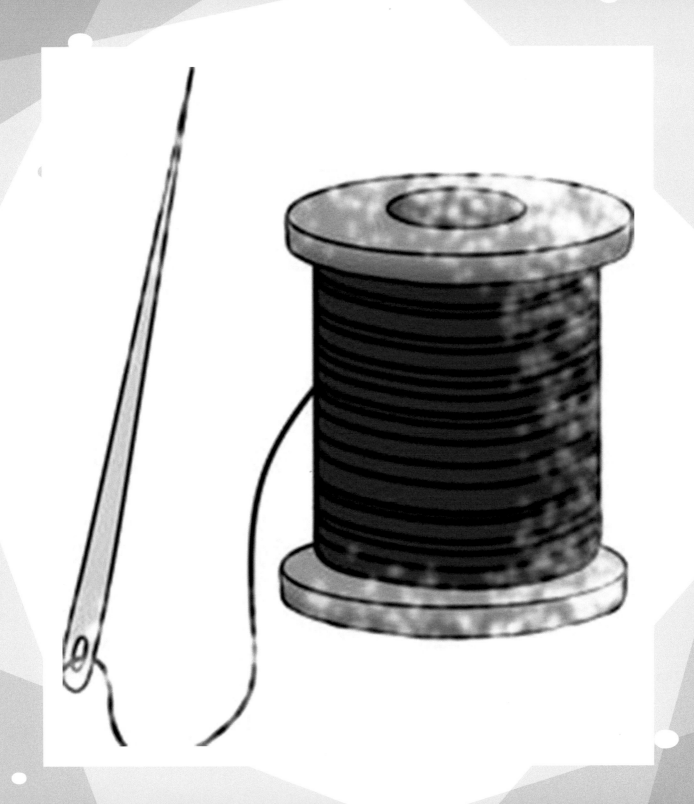

Later that day

all of the kingdom started to gather around to admire the prettiest tutu of all

time. Little did they know it was really a trap for Louie. Believe me he was around

cause you could smell him but you couldn't see. It was hard to tell where he was

the whole kingdom was everywhere trying to get a good look at the tutu.

Princess Leah Tutu and Freddy was waiting for Louie the looter, didn't you know it sure enough he was sneaking through a side entrance that was supposed to be sealed.

Louie knew his way around the castle for sure because he after all was the one who took the princess tutu's. So, Princess Leah tutu and Freddy hid into one of her closet's and waited for Louie to come. They were quiet as a mouse and Louie didn't know anyone was there. Louie just knew he was free and clear to steal the beautiful tutu. When he was just about to take the display out of the window,

out jumped Freddy and Princess Leah Tutu. Caught you red handed Louie the

looter, thought you could get away with another one didn't you. Yes, I'm caught

but you don't understand, I don't have all these beautiful things like the Princess

have.

There once was a time when I had similar things just like you and now I'm

less fortunate and no one would ever take a second look at me. One day I decided

I wanted to be a villager just like everyone else. I know they wouldn't want to be

Around me as I'm but as someone else they wouldn't mind. So I started taking

things to look pretty and by the way my name is Louise not Louie.

I'm a girl. I took the shoes so my feet would look nice but they were too small. It's

not easy having troll feet. I took the stockings so my legs would look nice instead

lumpy green logs and the lace to make my hair look pretty It's a mess. Princess

Leah I only took your tutu's because I knew how the made you feel and look.

I wanted to feel pretty to.

I really didn't mean any harm but I don't have anything anymore. Stealing is not

the way you should want to get things said Princess Leah Tutu. You were wrong

these things mean something to everyone. The shoe maker cannot seal shoes if

he does not have them. Lacey will not be able to seal her items as well. Poor

Mr. Buckley cannot seal bread if there is none. By the why, what's with the bread said Freddy why bread Louis? I was hungry so I took it. Your right Princess I didn't think about it like that I was only thinking about myself. I had forgotten all That I was taught for selfish reasons please forgive me Princess Leah Tutu. I am very ashamed of my behavior I was not brought up this way. I'm afraid I have to turn you in Louis and all the things you have stolen need to be returned to it's rightful owners said the princess. I know said Louis but before you do that may

I at least try on that amazing tutu because I never saw something so beautiful

in my life. What could it hurt said Freddy after all she came all this way maybe,

Yes you may said Princess Tutu and wouldn't you know it Louis was turned back

Into a princess again. Princess Tutu could not believe her eyes, oh my how could

this be you're a princess too.

My family was once royal and a witch cast an awful

spell on my us do to greed and we lost everything. It was only few years ago that

my father had past and I became alone and had to take care of myself that's the

real reason why I took things. Princess Louise I've heard stories of your family and

thought they were fairy tales I'm so sorry. Please don't apologize I'm the one who took what was not mine it's totally my fault. You should be able to tell your story

Princess Louise you must so the people would understand why you did what you

had to survive. But It's been so long since I've face a crowd I'm afraid they may

judge me for all my faults. With my help and mine too said Freddy we can do it

together. I thought you were turning me into the king. Not today Princess Louise today is your lucky day. You see I believe when you opened up and told the truth

you freed yourself from shame and exile. Your dress was magical, it brought me

back to who I truly am. Thank you Princess Leah Tutu and Freddy the finder frog

from the bottom of my heart. From now on we will be truly best friends and

share our live as such. Thank you for showing me there's more to me than just

beautiful tutu's.

P. S. Stories don't always turn out the way you expect them to.

When they are fairy tales anything can happen just open up your

mind and let your imagination run wild.

The End

By **L. Simmons Lee**

Printed in the United States
By Bookmasters